W9-DET-291

Here's what kids have to say to
Mary Pope Osborne, author of
the Magic Tree House series:

Your books are the best thing that ever happened to me.—Dash W.

I think kids of all ages should enjoy these books.—Missy C.

Even though I'm 11 and enjoy classic literature, I still sneak one of my brother's Jack and Annie books just for fun.—Gail R.

Thanks for inspiring me to read and write!
—Aaron B.

You are the best author who writes the best books in the world and that's the truth. I know it, you know it, and everybody knows it.
—Sarangen K.

When I read one of your books, I feel hypnotized. They are so spellbinding...I'm now going into grade 6, but I will still read them.—Ava V.

I'm sure that I'm speaking for all kids when I say we love your books.—Zach M.

Parents and teachers love
Magic Tree House books, too!

I have been teaching children to read for 32 years and have NEVER seen such a response to a series of books as I have to your Magic Tree House books. Every type of reader in my classroom, including learning-disabled, reluctant, and enrichment readers, has become obsessed with your books.
—V. Waller

My class is under the "spell" of the Magic Tree House. This is my fifth year of teaching, and I have never had an entire class so intrigued by one series of books.—B. Nyberg

We love your books! In our classroom reading program we have developed many units using your books. We do a "castle unit" around <u>The Knight at Dawn</u> as well as a "snow unit" using <u>Polar Bears Past Bedtime</u>.—D. Feltmeyer

I look forward to continuing to build my Magic Tree House library. Keep up the fantastic writing. Your characters Jack, Annie, and Morgan have taken on a life of their own!—D. Bean

I have to tell you that my students absolutely love your stories....[They] are also learning geography and history through the adventures of Jack and Annie.—A. Hamm

What a tribute it is to you as an author to get a bunch of 7-year-old boys so charged up about reading. Another mother and I were amazed that our sons begged us to buy your books instead of footballs.
—J. Sullivan

Dear Readers,

Years ago, I spent several months in India and found it to be a spectacularly colorful and interesting country. So it was a great joy for me to go back there in my imagination as I worked on _Tigers at Twilight_.

I also did research closer to home. To learn more about tigers, I visited the world-famous Bronx Zoo, in New York City. There I saw some magnificent tigers, and I learned that tigers are in danger of disappearing from the earth because so many are being killed by poachers. Many great zoos around the country help educate people about the need to protect wild animals.

As I wrote this book, the plight of the tiger greatly touched my heart. I hope it will touch yours, too. I also hope that people around the world will work together quickly to save these fierce and beautiful animals.

All my best,

Mary Pope Osborne

Tigers at Twilight

by
Mary Pope Osborne

illustrated by
Sal Murdocca

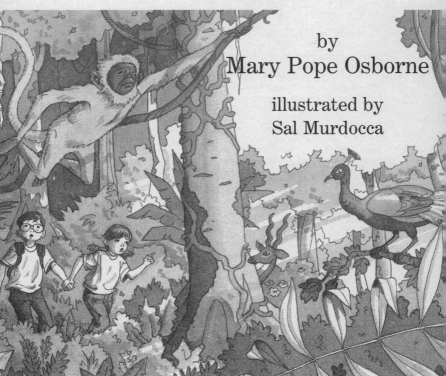

A STEPPING STONE BOOK™

Random House 🏠 New York

For Joy La Brack,
with gratitude for all her help

Text copyright © 1999 by Mary Pope Osborne.
Illustrations copyright © 1999 by Sal Murdocca.

www.randomhouse.com/kids
www.randomhouse.com/magictreehouse

Library of Congress Cataloging-in-Publication Data

Osborne, Mary Pope.
Tigers at twilight / by Mary Pope Osborne ; illustrated by Sal Murdocca.
p. cm. — (Magic tree house ; #19) "A Stepping Stone book."
SUMMARY: Having used their magic tree house to travel to India, where they must get a gift to help free the dog Teddy from a spell, Jack and Annie have adventures involving a tiger and other endangered jungle animals.
ISBN 0-679-89065-3 (trade) — ISBN 0-679-99065-8 (lib. bdg.)
[1. India—Fiction. 2. Dogs—Fiction. 3. Tigers—Fiction.
4. Jungle animals—Fiction. 5. Endangered species—Fiction.
6. Space and time—Fiction. 7. Magic—Fiction. 8. Tree houses—Fiction.]
I. Murdocca, Sal, ill. II. Title. III. Series: Osborne, Mary Pope. Magic tree house series ; #19. PZ7.O81167Ti 1999 [Fic]—dc21 99-23493

Printed in the United States of America 40 39

Random House, Inc.   New York, Toronto, London, Sydney, Auckland

Contents

Tyger! Tyger! burning bright
In the forests of the night;
What immortal hand or eye
Could frame thy fearful symmetry?

In what distant deeps or skies
Burnt the fire of thine eyes?
On what wings dare he aspire?
What the hand dare seize the fire?

—From *The Tyger* by William Blake, 1794

Prologue

One summer day in Frog Creek, Pennsylvania, a mysterious tree house appeared in the woods.

Eight-year-old Jack and his seven-year-old sister, Annie, climbed into the tree house. They found that it was filled with books.

Jack and Annie soon discovered that the tree house was magic. It could take them to the places in the books. All they had to do was point to a picture and wish to go there.

Along the way, Jack and Annie discovered

that the tree house belongs to Morgan le Fay. Morgan is a magical librarian from the time of King Arthur. She travels through time and space, gathering books.

In Magic Tree House Books #5–8, Jack and Annie helped free Morgan from a spell. In Books #9–12, they solved four ancient riddles and became Master Librarians.

In Magic Tree House Books #13–16, Jack and Annie had to save four ancient stories from being lost forever.

In Magic Tree House Books #17–20, Jack and Annie must be given four special gifts to help free an enchanted dog from a spell. They have already received a gift on a trip to the *Titanic* and a gift from the Lakota Indians. Now they are about to set out in search of the third gift . . .

1

How Far Away?

Jack and Annie walked past the Frog Creek woods on their way home from the library.

"I miss Teddy," said Annie.

"Me, too," said Jack.

"He's a really smart dog," said Annie.

"Yeah," said Jack, "and brave."

"And wise," said Annie.

"And funny," said Jack.

"And here!" said Annie.

"What?" said Jack.

"*Here!*" Annie pointed at the Frog Creek woods.

A small dog with tan-colored fur was peeking out from the bushes.

Arf! Arf! he barked.

"Oh, wow! Teddy!" said Jack.

The little dog ran off into the woods.

"Let's go!" said Annie.

She and Jack raced after Teddy. The Frog Creek woods glowed with late afternoon sunlight.

The dog ran between the trees and finally

stopped at a rope ladder. It hung from the tallest oak tree and led up to the magic tree house.

Teddy waited for Jack and Annie to catch up. He panted and wagged his tail.

"Hi, you!" cried Annie. She picked up the little dog and hugged him. "We missed you!"

"Yeah, silly!" said Jack. He kissed Teddy. Teddy licked his face.

"Is it time to get our *third* gift?" asked Annie.

Teddy sneezed, as if to say, *Of course!*

Annie grabbed the rope ladder and started up. Jack put Teddy inside his backpack and followed.

They climbed into the tree house. There was the note from Morgan le Fay. It was on the floor, just where it had been two days ago.

Jack let Teddy out of his pack.

Annie picked up the note and read:

This little dog is under a spell and needs your help. To free him, you must be given four special things:

A gift from a ship lost at sea,
A gift from the prairie blue,
A gift from a forest far away,
A gift from a kangaroo.

Be wise. Be brave. Be careful.
                    Morgan

Jack touched the first two gifts, which they had already gotten: a pocket watch from the *Titanic* and an eagle's feather from the Lakota Indians of the Great Plains.

"Now we have to get the gift from a forest far away," said Annie.

"I wonder *how* far away?" said Jack.

"I know how to find out," said Annie. "Where's our book?"

She and Jack looked around the tree house for one of the research books that Morgan always left them.

Arf! Arf! Teddy pawed a book in the corner.

Jack picked it up and read the title: *Wildlife of India.*

"Oh, man. India," he said. "That's *very* far away."

"Let's get going," said Annie, "so we can free Teddy."

Jack pointed at the cover of the book.

"I wish we could go there," he said.

The wind started to blow.

The tree house started to spin.

It spun faster and faster.

Then everything was still.

Absolutely still.

But only for a moment…

2

Kah and Ko

The warm air burst with sound.

Kah-ko!

Eee-eee!

Akkk-awkk!

"What's going on?" said Jack.

He and Annie looked out the window.

The sky was lit by an orange glow as the sun went down.

The tree house was in a tree by a stream at the edge of a forest.

The wild screeching and cawing came from the forest's tall, leafy trees.

Just then, two creatures leaped onto the windowsill.

"Aaah!" Jack and Annie yelled, jumping back.

Annie burst out laughing.

Arf! Arf! Teddy barked.

Two small monkeys peered at them. Their dark faces were framed with light gray fur. They looked as if they were wearing tiny parkas.

"Hi," said Annie. "I'm Annie. He's Jack. And he's Teddy. What are your names?"

Kah-ko, kah-ko, the monkeys chattered.

"Cool," said Annie. She turned to Jack. "Her name is Kah. His name is Ko."

"Oh, brother," said Jack.

"I bet he *is* her brother," said Annie.

Kah and Ko whooped as if laughing at Annie's joke. Their yellow eyes twinkled.

"We came to get a gift from the forest," said Annie. "Do you know where we can find it?"

The monkeys nodded and chattered. Then they started down the tree.

Using their long tails and arms, they swung from branch to branch. They jumped to the ground and looked up.

"Coming! Bring Teddy, Jack," Annie said. Then she started down the ladder.

Jack quickly flipped through *Wildlife of India*. He found a picture of the gray monkeys. He read:

> **This monkey is called a langur (say lun-GOOR). The word *langur* means "having a long tail."**

Jack pulled his notebook and pencil out of his backpack. He wrote:

langur means long tail

Annie's laughter came from below. It blended with the sounds of the forest.

Arf! Arf! barked Teddy.

"Okay, okay," said Jack.

He put the book, his notebook, and Teddy into his pack. Then he hurried down the ladder.

Annie was playing with the langurs on the stream bank.

Jack put Teddy on the ground.

Kah bounded over to Jack and grabbed his hand. The langur's paw felt like a tiny human hand.

Kah pulled Jack toward the forest. Ko

14

pulled Annie, and Teddy scampered after them.

The langurs climbed the huge, leafy trees. Then they began swinging from branch to branch, like kids on a jungle gym.

Annie dashed beneath the swinging monkeys. Teddy ran after her.

"Wait, wait!" Jack called, hurrying after them all. "Annie, slow down! We don't know anything about this place."

The langurs slowed down, as if they understood Jack's words. Jack caught up with Annie. They walked on through the forest.

"This is so amazing," said Annie.

Jack agreed.

The sunset gave the trees a fiery glow.

The hot air smelled sweet.

Blue peacocks spread their tails.
Yellow birds flew from tree to tree.
Small deer ate red flowers in a clearing.
"It's like paradise," said Annie.

"Yeah, but don't forget the title of our book: *Wildlife of India*," said Jack. "'Wildlife' means scary animals, too."

Jack noticed long, deep gashes in a tree as they walked by. He stopped.

"What happened there?" he said.

Annie shrugged and kept walking.

Jack pulled the book out of his pack. There was a picture of a tree with gashes.

He read aloud:

> **Tigers sharpen their claws on tree trunks. They leave big gashes in the bark.**

"What?" said Annie. She stopped and looked back at the tree.

"See what I mean?" said Jack. "Tigers live here. And one of them just came this way."

3

Life or Death

"Tigers?" said Annie. "Cool."

Jack read more:

> A wild tiger eats almost 5,000 pounds
> of fresh raw meat a year.

"Oh, not so cool," said Annie.

Jack went on:

> Tigers usually leave elephants alone.
> And like many smaller cats, tigers
> often avoid wild dogs.

19

Teddy growled.

"*Wild* dogs, not a shrimp like you," Jack said to Teddy. "A tiger would eat you in a minute."

Teddy growled again.

Just then, Kah and Ko began hooting. *Koo-koo-koo!*

The peacocks cried *Kok! Kok!*

The small deer made short barking sounds and stamped their hooves.

"What's going on?" said Annie.

"We better put Teddy in my pack," said Jack, "to keep him safe."

Jack slipped the dog into his pack. Teddy's head poked out the top.

"All set?" Jack asked the little dog.

Teddy growled again.

This time, a deep, fierce growl answered

back. It seemed to surround them.

Jack's hair stood on end.

"Yikes!" said Annie.

"A tiger!" said Jack.

Arf! Arf! Teddy barked.

Kah and Ko screeched at Jack and Annie from their tree.

"They want us to join them!" said Annie. "Come on!" She grabbed a branch and climbed up.

Jack's hands were shaking as he put his backpack on. He grabbed a branch and pushed off the ground. He pulled himself into the tree.

Another growl shook the forest.

"Oh, man," said Jack.

Koo-koo-koo! The langurs climbed higher up the tree.

Jack and Annie followed them, climbing from branch to branch.

The sky above was no longer glowing. The bright orange had faded to a twilight gray.

Jack looked down. He couldn't see the ground at all.

He listened for another scary roar.

Only the cries of frightened forest creatures filled the air.

"Maybe the tiger's gone," said Annie.

Jack glanced at Kah and Ko. The langurs cuddled together. Their dark faces looked worried.

"And maybe *not*," said Jack.

"How can we get through the forest without running into him?" said Annie.

"That's a problem," said Jack. "And it's

getting dark. Soon we won't be able to see anything."

Kah and Ko hooted again. They pointed down the tree trunk.

Arf! Arf! Teddy barked from Jack's pack.

"Do they see the tiger?" Jack asked, his heart thumping again. He couldn't see anything but leaves and branches.

Then, far below, he saw the tree trunk *move!*

"A snake!" said Annie.

The snake was slithering around the trunk. It had black-and-tan markings. The snake's body was as thick as the tree trunk!

"*A python,*" breathed Jack.

The python kept curling up the tree trunk.

"Is it poisonous?" asked Annie.

Jack pulled out their book. By the last light of

day, he found a picture of a python. He read aloud:

The python is not a poisonous snake.

"Whew," said Annie.

"Not so fast," said Jack. He read more:

To kill its prey, the python squeezes it to death, then swallows it whole. A python can swallow an animal the size of a full-grown deer.

"Oh, yuck!" said Annie.

"This is more than just *yuck*, Annie," said Jack. "This is life or death."

Kah and Ko chattered at Jack and Annie.

"Not now," said Jack. "We have to think."

The langurs grabbed thick vines. They leaned back. Then they jumped out of the tree!

25

The langurs swung through the air like trapeze artists. They swung over bushes and tall grass and landed in another tree.

They screeched at Jack and Annie and waved their arms.

"I know what they're saying," said Annie. "They want us to copy them!"

4

Swing Time

Annie grabbed a vine.

Jack looked back at the python. The giant snake was still winding its way up the tree. It had almost reached their branch.

Jack took a deep breath. Then he grabbed a vine, too.

"Lean back, like Kah and Ko did," said Annie.

Jack and Annie leaned back.

"One, two, three—go!" said Annie.

They swung out of the tree.

Jack felt his stomach drop. Air rushed by. Leaves and branches slapped at him.

Suddenly, the forest shook with a great roar.

Like a flame, a tiger leaped up from the bushes!

His yellow eyes blazed. His teeth shone like daggers. His claws barely missed Jack and Annie!

"AAAHHH!" they yelled.

The tiger crashed back down into the bushes.

Jack and Annie swung into the langurs' tree.

Jack threw one leg around the trunk. He let go of his vine and held on tightly to a branch.

"Oh, man!" he said. He was in shock.

The langurs patted him, as if to make sure he was okay.

"Wow, that was fun," said Annie, sitting on a big branch.

"Fun? Are you nuts?" said Jack.

"The *swinging* was fun," said Annie. "The tiger was scary."

Just then, the tree began to shake. Branches snapped below.

"Oh, no!" said Jack.

"Can tigers climb trees?" asked Annie.

"Probably," said Jack. He hugged the trunk and squeezed his eyes shut.

From below came loud sounds of chewing, smacking, and crunching.

Teddy growled.

Jack groaned.

"Now the tiger's *eating* the tree," he said.

Annie burst into laughter.

Kah and Ko whooped as if they were laughing, too.

Arf! Arf! barked Teddy.

"What?" said Jack, opening his eyes.

"Look!" Annie pointed at the twilight.

A thick gray tube was waving in the air.

"Another snake?" said Jack, horrified.

"No! An elephant trunk!" said Annie.

The trunk wiggled near Jack and Annie, as if it were sniffing them. Then it picked leaves from the tree and disappeared.

"Let's go see!" said Annie.

With Teddy still in his backpack, Jack followed Annie down to a lower branch.

They peered out at the twilight forest.

In the gray gloom, they saw a herd of elephants.

One stood beneath their tree, eating leaves. Others munched grass.

"Hey, I've got a really cool idea," said Annie.

31

5

Night Walk

"Uh-oh," said Jack. "What is it?"

"I know how to escape the tiger," said Annie. "Our book said tigers don't attack elephants, right?"

"Yeah," said Jack.

"So we should travel through the forest on the back of an elephant," said Annie.

Jack nodded slowly.

"That *is* a cool idea," he said. "But—"

"No buts. I'll get on first," said Annie.

She climbed down the tree until she was close to the elephant's back. She carefully lowered herself off a branch. When her feet rested on the elephant's back, she let go of the branch. Then she slowly sat down.

The elephant let out a low rumbling sound and shifted her weight.

"Don't worry, it's just me," Annie said softly. She patted the huge creature's back. "Thanks, Saba."

"Saba?" said Jack.

"That's her name," said Annie. "She just told me."

"Yeah, right," said Jack.

Arf! Arf! barked Teddy.

"Come on, Jack," said Annie. "It's not scary."

Jack sighed and slowly climbed down the

tree. When he was above Saba, he lowered himself off the branch.

He put both feet on the elephant. Then he carefully sat down in front of Annie.

Saba rumbled again.

"Tell her not to worry," said Annie. "Pat her head."

"Don't worry, Saba," Jack said. He patted

the elephant's head. Her skin was rough and wrinkled.

The elephant curled her trunk back and rested it on Jack's head.

"Hi," he said in a small voice.

Saba flapped her ears.

Kah and Ko swung to the ground in front of Saba. They chattered at her. She waved her trunk at them. The langurs began bounding through the forest.

Saba followed.

The rest of the herd followed in line. Saba walked with a calm, rolling motion. Jack felt as if he were riding over ocean waves.

A full moon was rising above the trees.

"Where are we going?" Jack asked.

"Just relax," said Annie. "Kah and Ko know where to go."

Arf! Arf! Teddy barked from Jack's backpack.

"You relax, too," Jack said to the little dog.

Fireflies blinked. The moon lit a path between the trees as the elephants marched on.

From a distance came a low growl.

Is that the tiger? Jack wondered.

The elephants paid no attention. They kept walking through the warm woods. They marched slowly under hanging vines and through misty clearings.

Kah and Ko bounded ahead of them, two moon shadows leading the way.

"We're going far from the tree house," said Jack.

"Don't worry," Annie said.

Suddenly, a long roar split the night.

A chill went down Jack's spine.

The roar came again. It turned into a yowling. The yowling turned into steady moaning. It sounded as if the whole forest were moaning.

"That's a really sad sound," said Annie sleepily.

"Yeah," said Jack.

But the elephants all marched on.

Jack rocked in sleepy rhythm with Saba's walk. He could hear Teddy snoring in his backpack.

Soon Jack's head rested on Saba's back. He began drifting in and out of dreams— dreams of rocking in a boat under the dark treetops.

6

Swamp Creature

Caw! Caw!

Awk! Awk! Awk!

Jack slowly came out of his dream. He opened his eyes with a start.

He was surrounded by hazy sunlight.

Where am I? he thought in a panic.

Then he remembered—he was in India, on an elephant's back!

He sat up. Through the haze, he saw that Saba was standing on a muddy stream bank.

Jack yawned. Where was Annie?

The other elephants were upstream. They sprayed water on each other with their trunks.

Teddy, Kah, and Ko were at the edge of the forest. Teddy sniffed the tall grass. The langurs ate flowers.

"Good morning!" called Annie.

She was sitting on a big black rock downstream. She was barefoot and soaking wet.

"Hi," said Jack. "How did you get down?"

"Teddy and I slid off Saba into the mud," said Annie. "Try it. But throw down your sneakers and backpack first."

Annie went to Saba's side. Her feet were buried in mud up to her ankles.

Jack threw his things to Annie. Then he patted Saba's rough, wrinkled skin.

"Thanks for the ride," he said softly.

The elephant touched him one last time with her trunk.

Jack slid down her side—feet first—and fell into the mud. He caught himself with his hands. They sank into the mud past his wrists. His glasses were spattered, too.

"Wash off in the stream," Annie said.

She put Jack's pack and shoes on the rock while Jack waded into the cool water.

He washed the mud off his hands and feet. He rinsed off his glasses. Then he looked around.

Saba had joined the rest of the herd. The elephants looked beautiful in the morning mist.

Everything looked beautiful.

Yellow and blue water birds spread their

wings. Mossy hanging vines swayed in the breeze. Huge white flowers floated on top of the stream.

Then Jack saw a strange sight. It looked like a horn and two ears sticking out of the water. One ear flicked away a fly.

"There's a weird creature out here," he called to Annie. "It looks like it has a horn."

Annie waded into the stream.

"I better check the book," said Jack.

He hurried to his pack, wiping his wet hands on his T-shirt. He pulled out the India book.

There was a picture of a horn sticking out of the water. He read:

> **The one-horned rhinoceros, or "rhino,"**
> **washes in a forest stream. Rhinos are**
> **not usually dangerous. But because**

> they do not see well, they sometimes
> charge at things by mistake. A loud
> noise will usually stop them.

Jack felt sorry for the rhinos. *Too bad animals can't wear glasses*, he thought. He read more:

> The Indian rhino is a very endangered
> animal. This means that there are not
> many left. People called poachers kill
> them and sell their body parts as medi-
> cine and good-luck charms.

Jack started to take out his notebook.

Just then, a slurpy, sloshing sound came from the water.

"Whoa!" said Annie.

Jack looked up.

The rhino rose from the stream. He looked like an ancient swamp creature.

"Oh, man!" said Jack.

The rhino peered at Annie with his tiny eyes.

Then he snorted and lowered his head. His horn pointed right at Annie.

"Make a loud noise!" Jack yelled.

Annie clapped her hands and shouted, "We come in peace!"

The rhino stopped. He grunted. Then he sank back into the water.

Annie laughed.

"Whew," said Jack. "I better take some

notes about that big guy."

Arf! Arf! Teddy barked from the edge of the forest.

"And I better get Teddy," said Annie.

She hurried out of the stream and ran to get the dog. Jack pulled out his notebook and wrote:

<u>One-horned rhino</u>

an endangered animal

needs glasses

"Jack!" shouted Annie. She was racing toward him, with Teddy at her heels. "Come quick!"

"What's wrong?" he said.

"We found something terrible!" Annie was close to tears. "*Really* terrible!"

7

Trapped!

Jack threw his things into his pack and followed Annie to the forest edge.

Teddy stayed close to them, whining. Kah and Ko bounced around, chattering nervously.

As Jack got closer, he saw a tiger. The tiger was lying on his side, completely still. His eyes were closed. His front paw was caught in a trap.

"Is he dead?" said Jack.

"No, he's still breathing," Annie said. A tear ran down her cheek. "He's worn out from struggling. He must have gotten caught last night. That's the sad sound we heard."

"What can we do?" said Jack.

"We have to free him!" said Annie. She started toward the tiger.

"Wait! Wait!" Jack grabbed her. "Tigers eat people, you know." He took a deep breath. "Let's see what the book says first."

"Hurry," said Annie.

Jack opened their India book. He found a chapter called "Tiger Traps." He read:

> **Poachers catch Indian tigers with steel traps. This is against the law. After trapping a tiger, they kill it and sell the body parts for money. Like the rhino, the tiger is a very endangered species.**

If the killing does not end, they both face extinction. Extinction means that someday there may be no Indian tigers or rhinos left on earth.

"Oh, man, we *do* have to save him," said Jack.

Under the writing was a picture of a steel trap used to catch tigers. Jack studied it. It looked horrible and deadly.

"Okay," he said. He showed the picture to Annie. "Here's the plan. I'll push down on this part. The trap will spring open. Then you pull his leg out. Got it?"

"Got it," said Annie. "Sit, Teddy."

The little dog sat.

The langurs watched silently as Jack and Annie moved closer to the tiger.

He was the most majestic creature Jack

had ever seen. His huge head was a dark orange color. He had perfect black-and-white stripes around his wide face.

The leg in the ugly steel trap was bleeding.

Slowly, silently, Jack pushed down the lever.

He raised the bar off the tiger's leg.

The tiger kept sleeping.

Slowly, silently, Annie freed the tiger's leg. She stroked his fur gently.

"Get well," she whispered.

The tiger didn't move.

Slowly, silently, Jack and Annie stood up.

They turned around. They started tiptoeing
back toward the langurs.

Koo-koo-koo! warned Kah and Ko.

Jack and Annie turned back.

The tiger was on his feet. He stared right at them. His eyes seemed to glow.

Jack looked about wildly. How could they escape?

The tiger snarled at Jack and Annie.

Then slowly, silently, he started toward them.

8

Wonder Dog

The huge tiger limped closer and closer to Jack and Annie.

Jack clapped his hands.

"We come in peace!" he shouted.

But the tiger didn't turn away. His eyes blazed. His lip curled.

Arf! Arf! Teddy barked fiercely at Annie.

"Teddy says run and hide!" said Annie.

She grabbed Jack's hand and pulled him over to the bank.

"Wait—what about Teddy?" he cried.

"Don't worry!" Annie said.

She pulled Jack down behind the black rock.

"What about Teddy?" Jack asked again.

"He's okay—he told me!" said Annie.

Jack heard Teddy's barks turn to fierce growls.

ARF! ARF! GRRR! GRRRR!

The growls grew louder and louder.

"That doesn't sound like Teddy," said Jack.

Then suddenly, there was silence. A strange silence.

"Teddy?" Annie asked. Now *she* sounded worried.

Annie raised her head. She and Jack both peered over the rock.

Teddy stood tall and brave in the grass.

The tiger was limping away. He disappeared between the trees.

All the forest seemed to hold its breath—until Annie broke the silence.

"Teddy, you're a wonder dog!" she said.

The langurs clapped and jumped up and down.

Arf! Arf! Teddy was just like a small scruffy dog again. He wagged his tail and ran to Annie and Jack.

Annie scooped him into her arms.

"You saved us!" she said.

"How did you drive away that tiger?" asked Jack, rubbing Teddy's head. "Did you turn into a wild dog?"

Teddy just panted and licked them both.

Jack pushed his glasses into place and looked back at the forest.

"Well, I guess we won't be getting a thank-you gift from that tiger," he said.

Annie laughed.

"I guess not," she said. "I wonder where our gift is."

"And I wonder where the tree house is," said Jack.

Kah and Ko chattered at Jack. Then they bounded down the bank, waving their arms.

"They want us to follow them again," said Annie. "Come on."

She and Jack grabbed their things off the rock. They hurried down the stream after the langurs.

The water shimmered in the early light. Silver fish leaped into the air.

Teddy bounded ahead with Kah and Ko. Soon they disappeared around a bend.

Jack and Annie followed them.

When they went around the bend, they

saw a man sitting cross-legged on a rock. The langurs sat close to him.

The man's eyes were closed.

He had long white hair and a long white beard. His skin was brown.

He looked *very* peaceful.

9

The Hermit

Kah and Ko smoothed the man's hair with their little paws and patted his cheeks gently.

The man smiled and whispered to the langurs. His eyes stayed closed.

Teddy walked up to the man and licked his hands.

The man still didn't open his eyes. But he stroked Teddy's fur.

"Knock, knock," Annie said softly.

"Is someone there?" the man asked.

He turned his face toward Jack and Annie. Now his eyes were open, but he did not seem to see them. Jack realized that the man was blind.

"Hi, I'm Annie," said Annie.

"And I'm Jack," said Jack.

The blind man smiled.

"Good," he said, nodding. "Would you like to visit with me?"

"Sure," said Annie.

She and Jack sat down next to the man.

"Do you live in this forest?" Annie asked.

"Yes," he said.

"Are you a hermit?" Jack asked.

"Yes," the blind man said.

"What's a hermit?" said Annie.

"Hermits live far away from other people," said the blind man. "We like to be alone to think. I live in the forest so I can learn from nature."

"How do you learn?" asked Jack.

"I listen," said the blind man.

"Listen to what?" asked Jack.

"To the chatter of the monkeys, the rumble of the elephant, the roar of the tiger," said the man. "I have listened for so long, they have all begun to sound like one voice—the one great voice of the forest."

"Did the voice tell you that a tiger got caught in a trap last night?" asked Annie.

"Yes," the hermit said.

"And did it tell you that after we saved him, he tried to attack us?" said Jack.

The blind man smiled.

"Please bring me one of the white flowers floating on the stream," he said.

Jack wondered why the hermit was changing the subject.

But Annie jumped up and hurried to the stream. She pulled at one of the large flowers. It came up, muddy root and all. She took it to the blind man.

"Thank you," he said.

The man touched the flower's large white petals and its dirty root.

"This perfect lotus blossom grows from dark, thick mud," he said. "Its beauty cannot live without its ugliness. Do you understand?"

"Yes," said Jack and Annie.

"When you saved the tiger, you saved *all* of him," said the blind man. "You saved his graceful beauty—*and* his fierce, savage nature. You cannot have one without the other."

"Oh…right," said Jack.

"Take this lotus as a thank-you gift from all the forest for saving our fierce friend," said the blind man. "Our world would not be complete without him."

Annie took the gift from the hermit.

"A gift from a forest far away," she said.

Arf! Arf! Teddy wagged his tail.

The langurs clapped.

"We can go home now," said Jack, "if we can just find the way."

"Do not worry," said the blind man. "Your house in the trees is close by. The elephants walked in a large circle. So you are back at the place where you started."

"Really?" said Jack.

The blind man pointed to the sky.

There was the magic tree house, high in a nearby tree.

"Oh, great," breathed Jack.

"I told you not to worry," said Annie. She and Jack pulled on their socks and shoes and stood up.

Before they left, Annie touched the hand of the blind man.

"Thanks for everything," she said.

The man held her hand for a moment. Then he took Jack's hand. Jack felt a wave of calm wash over him.

"Thank you," he said to the blind man.

Kah and Ko chattered and held out their long arms. Jack and Annie hugged the two langurs.

"We'll miss you," said Annie.

"You were great tour guides," said Jack. "Good-bye."

Then he and Annie took off for the magic tree house with Teddy scampering after them.

At the rope ladder, Jack put Teddy into his pack and climbed up.

Annie carried the lotus blossom as she followed them.

Inside the tree house, Jack picked up the Pennsylvania book. But before he made a wish, he looked out the window with Annie.

In the distance, they saw Saba and the other elephants bathing in the stream.

They saw Kah and Ko swinging on vines.

They saw the tiger sunbathing in the grass, licking his sore leg.

They saw tiny deer grazing.

They saw bright birds in the trees.

They saw the blind man sitting in front of his cave. He was smiling.

Jack opened the book. He pointed to a picture of the Frog Creek woods.

"I wish we could go home," he said.

The tree house started to spin.

The wind started to blow.

It blew harder and harder.

Then everything was still.

Absolutely still.

10

Who Are You, Really?

Jack opened his eyes.

Late afternoon sunlight shined into the tree house.

"Our third gift," said Annie.

She put the lotus blossom beside the pocket watch from the *Titanic* and the eagle's feather from the Lakota Indians.

"One more gift," she said to Teddy, "and you'll be free from your spell."

The little dog licked her hand.

"Hey, tell me this," said Jack. "How did you know Teddy wanted us to hide behind that rock?"

Annie shrugged.

"I just knew," she said. "I think I saw it in his eyes."

"You *did?*" Jack looked into Teddy's eyes.

The little dog tilted his head and stared back at Jack.

Teddy's eyes twinkled, as if they held many secrets.

"Who are you, really?" whispered Jack.

Teddy just smiled a doggy smile and wagged his tail.

"Come for us again soon," Annie said. "Okay?"

Teddy sneezed, as if to say, *Of course!*

Jack grabbed his pack. Then he and

Annie climbed down the rope ladder.

When they stood on the ground, they looked up. A little black nose was poking out the tree house window.

"Bye!" they called.

Arf! Arf!

Jack and Annie took off between the trees.

Birds sang in the twilight. Squirrels scampered playfully through the leaves.

The Frog Creek woods were very tame after the forest in India.

Soon they came to their street. As they walked to their house, the last bit of daylight was slipping away.

Before they went inside, Jack and Annie sat on their steps.

"I have two questions," said Jack. "If the hermit couldn't see, how did he know about the tree house? And how did he know that we had traveled all night with the elephants?"

"Easy," said Annie. "The one great voice of the forest told him."

"Hmm," said Jack.

He closed his eyes for a moment and listened.

He heard a car going down the street.

He heard a woodpecker pecking.

He heard crickets chirping.

He heard a screen door opening.

He heard a mom saying, "Time for dinner, kids."

All the sounds were like one great voice— the one great voice of home.

Around the World with Jack and Annie!

You have traveled to far away places and have been
on countless Magic Tree House adventures.
Now is your chance to receive an official
Magic Tree House passport and collect official stamps
for each destination from around the world!

HOW

Get your exclusive Magic Tree House Passport!*

Send your name, street address, city, state, zip code, and date of birth to:
The Magic Tree House Passport, Random House Children's Books,
Marketing Department, 1745 Broadway, 10th Floor, New York, NY 10019

OR log on to **www.magictreehouse.com/passport**
to download and print your passport now!

Collect Official Magic Tree House Stamps:

Log on to **www.magictreehouse.com** to submit your answers to the
trivia questions below. If you answer correctly, you will automatically
receive your official stamp for Book 19: *Tigers at Twilight*.

1. What kind of animal is a langur?

2. What kind of snake has black-and-tan markings?

**3. What is the name of the elephant
that Jack and Annie ride on?**

*One passport per person. No purchase necessary. While supplies last. Allow 6 to 8 weeks for delivery. Passports available beginning March 2007.

Read all the Magic Tree House adventures for a chance to collect them all!

MORE FACTS FOR YOU AND JACK

1) Adult elephants are plant eaters. They feed for 15 hours a day and can eat more than 400 pounds of vegetation every day.

2) The average weight of an Indian rhino is 4,000 pounds.

3) A giant python can grow up to 30 feet in length.

4) India has 238 kinds of snakes, ranging from the giant python to the worm snake, which is just over 4 inches long.

The Sacred Langur

Hinduism is the main religion of the people of India. It is a religion with many gods and goddesses. One of its important gods is Hanuman, who saved a Hindu goddess named Sita.

Hanuman has the body of a man and the face and tail of a langur monkey. Followers of Hinduism believe that Hanuman's spirit is alive in the langurs of India. Hindu temples dedicated to Hanuman treat all langurs as special guests.

Endangered Species

In the nineteenth century, there were more than 40,000 tigers in India. Today there are fewer than 4,000. For this reason, the tiger is considered to be a critically endangered species.

The Indian rhino is also a highly endangered species.

The Wildlife Protection Society of India has been formed to help save India's endangered animals. The society arrests illegal hunters and seizes wildlife products, such as tiger skins and bones, rhino horn, and elephant ivory. It also helps to alert other people around the world to India's wildlife crisis.

Don't miss the next Magic Tree House book,
in which Jack and Annie are whisked away
to the land of Australia...

MAGIC TREE HOUSE #20

DINGOES AT DINNERTIME

(January 2000)

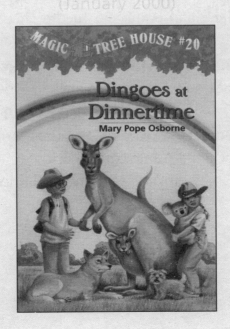

Where have you traveled in the

MAGIC TREE HOUSE?

The Mystery of the Tree House
(Books #1–4)

❑ **Magic Tree House #1, DINOSAURS BEFORE DARK,** in which Jack and Annie discover the tree house and travel back to the time of dinosaurs.

❑ **Magic Tree House #2, THE KNIGHT AT DAWN,** in which Jack and Annie go to the time of knights and explore a medieval castle with a hidden passage.

❑ **Magic Tree House #3, MUMMIES IN THE MORNING,** in which Jack and Annie go to ancient Egypt and get lost in a pyramid when they help a ghost queen.

❑ **Magic Tree House #4, PIRATES PAST NOON,** in which Jack and Annie travel back in time and meet some unfriendly pirates searching for buried treasure.

The Mystery of the Magic Spell
(Books #5–8)

❑ **Magic Tree House #5, NIGHT OF THE NINJAS,** in which Jack and Annie go to old Japan and learn the secrets of the ninjas.

❑ **Magic Tree House #6, AFTERNOON ON THE AMAZON,** in which Jack and Annie explore the wild rain forest of the Amazon and are greeted by army ants, crocodiles, and flesh-eating piranhas.

❑ **Magic Tree House #7, SUNSET OF THE SABER-TOOTH,** in which Jack and Annie go back to the Ice Age—the world of woolly mammoths, sabertooth tigers, and a mysterious sorcerer.

❑ **Magic Tree House #8, MIDNIGHT ON THE MOON,** in which Jack and Annie go forward in time and explore the moon in a moon buggy.

The Mystery of the Ancient Riddles
(Books #9–12)

❑ **Magic Tree House #9, DOLPHINS AT DAYBREAK,** in which Jack and Annie arrive on a coral reef, where they find a mini-submarine that takes them underwater into the world of sharks and dolphins.

❑ **Magic Tree House #10, GHOST TOWN AT SUNDOWN,** in which Jack and Annie travel to the Wild West, where they battle horse thieves, meet a kindly cowboy, and get some help from a mysterious ghost.

❑ **Magic Tree House #11, LIONS AT LUNCHTIME,** in which Jack and Annie go to the plains of Africa, where they help wild animals cross a rushing river and have a picnic with a Masai warrior.

❑ **Magic Tree House #12, POLAR BEARS PAST BEDTIME,** in which Jack and Annie go to the Arctic, where they get help from a seal hunter, play with polar bear cubs, and get trapped on thin ice.

The Mystery of the Lost Stories
(Books #13–16)

❏ **Magic Tree House #13, Vacation on the Volcano,** in which Jack and Annie land in Pompeii during Roman times, on the very day Mount Vesuvius erupts!

❏ **Magic Tree House #14, Day of the Dragon King,** in which Jack and Annie travel back to ancient China, where they must face an emperor who burns books.

❏ **Magic Tree House #15, Viking Ships at Sunrise,** in which Jack and Annie visit a monastery in medieval Ireland on the day the Vikings attack!

❏ **Magic Tree House #16, Hour of the Olympics,** in which Jack and Annie are whisked back to ancient Greece and the first Olympic games.

The Mystery of the Enchanted Dog
(Books #17–20)

❑ **Magic Tree House #17, TONIGHT ON THE TITANIC,** in which Jack and Annie travel back to the decks of the *Titanic* and help two children escape from the sinking ship.

❑ **Magic Tree House #18, BUFFALO BEFORE BREAKFAST,** in which Jack and Annie go back in time to the Great Plains, where they meet a Lakota boy and have to stop a buffalo stampede!

A STEPPING STONE BOOK™

Great authors write great books...
for fantastic first reading experiences!

Grades 1–3

Junie B. Jones series by Barbara Park
Magic Tree House series
   by Mary Pope Osborne
Marvin Redpost series by Louis Sachar
Space Dog series by Natalie Standiford

BABE: Going Quackers
BABE: Pigs and Robbers

Clyde Robert Bulla
The Chalk Box Kid
The Paint Brush Kid
White Bird

Jackie French Koller
Mole and Shrew All Year Through

Jerry Spinelli
Tooter Pepperday
Blue Ribbon Blues: A Tooter Tale

Sharon Dennis Wyeth
Ginger Brown: Too Many Houses
Ginger Brown: The Nobody Boy

Grades 2–4

A to Z Mysteries series by Ron Roy

Polly Berrien Berends
The Case of the Elevator Duck

Ann Cameron
Julian, Dream Doctor
Julian, Secret Agent
Julian's Glorious Summer

Adèle Geras
Little Swan

Paul Hindman and Nate Evans
Dragon Bones

Dean Hughes
Brad and Butter Play Ball!

**Stephanie Spinner &
Jonathan Etra**
Aliens for Breakfast
Aliens for Lunch
Aliens for Dinner

Gloria Whelan
Next Spring an Oriole
Silver
Hannah
Night of the Full Moon
Shadow of the Wolf

Grades 3–5

The Magic Elements Quartet
   by Mallory Loehr
#1: Water Wishes
#2: Earth Magic

Mary Pope Osborne
#1: Spider Kane and the Mystery Under the
   May-Apple
#2: Spider Kane and the Mystery at Jumbo
   Nightcrawler's